the daria diaries

by Anne D. Bernstein

MTV BOOKS   POCKET BOOKS

Writer: Anne D. Bernstein
Editor: Michele Tomasik
Art Direction/Reiner Design: Roger Gorman and Leah Sherman
Art Director/MTV: Karen Hyden
Production Coordinator: Sara Duffy
Artists: Kirk Etienne, Guy Moore, Craig Berman, Karen Disher, Eric Wight,
Olivia Ward, Brian Moyer, Jody Schaeffer, Miriam Kaitin

Color Supervisor: Olivia Ward
Color Designers: Amy Melson, Christine Costan, Laura Bryson, Donelle Estey
Cel Painters: Jarrett DeMartino, Linda Negron, Carla Snow
Production Assistants: Brent Thorn, David Trexler

Daria Creative Supervisors: Glenn Eichler, Susie Lewis Lynn

Special Thanks: Mike Baez, Eduardo A. Braniff, Cindy Brolsma, Lemon Krasny, Andrea Labate,
John Lynn, Brad MacDonald, Dominie Mahl, Kim Noone, Amy Palmer, Ed Paparo, Renee Presser,
Robin Silverman, Donald Silvey, Jen Stipcich, Machi Tantillo, Abby Terkuhle, Van Toffler, James D Wood

Special thanks at Pocket Books to: Lynda Castillo, Gina Centrello, Millicent Fairhurst,
Lisa Feuer, Max Greenhut, Donna O'Neill, Liate Stehlik, Dave Stern, and Kara Welsh.
Also thanks to Greg Wade at Color Associates.

This book is a work of fiction. Names, characters, places, and incidents are either
products of the author's imagination or are used fictitiously.

An Original Publication of MTV Books/Pocket Books

POCKET BOOKS, a division of Simon and Schuster, Inc.
1230 Avenue of the Americas, New York, NY 10020

ISBN: 0-671-01709-8

First MTV Books/Pocket Books trade paperback printing January 1998

10 9 8 7 6 5 4 3 2 1

Pocket and colophon are registered trademarks of Simon and Schuster Inc.

Printed in the U.S.A.

Left the town of Highland this morning with no regrets, looking forward to the move to Lawndale with excitement and anticipation. Then I remembered my family was coming too.

I felt the need to bring along a memento of my former life, so I removed the front doorknob when no one was looking and slipped it into my jacket pocket. I hope the new owners don't have their hearts set on a lot of going in and out.

Quinn had filled the car trunk and half the backseat with wardrobe overflow, so I had to ride in the moving van. The movers were pretty cool. They let me be the lookout while they stopped to run a quick errand in the warehouse district. When they got back, they offered me a new microwave oven as a token of their gratitude, but I said no. Sure, you tell yourself it'll be just for popcorn, but the next thing you know you're steaming fresh broccoli.

By the time we pulled up at the new house, Quinn had already claimed the so-called "normal" room. I was left to inhabit the room that had belonged to the former owner's schizophrenic mother. It's extremely creepy, with padded walls and sawed-off bars on the windows...as usual, my sister has played right into my hands. Mom says she's going to redecorate my room. Probably right after she gets around to signing my third-grade report card.

The house is bigger than our old one, which is good because it'll be easier to avoid Quinn. The phones are hooked up (the people who bought our old house already called up looking for their doorknob). And from what I've seen of Lawndale, it looks like a pleasant, typical suburban town. A nice place to raise a normal family.

Somebody please help me.

Welcome to Lawndale

1. CHEZ PIERRE
Real cloth napkins; fake French accents. Waiters snicker when someone uses the wrong fork.

2. CREWE NECK
Where nobody mows their own lawn, mops their own floor, or colors their own hair in the sink.

3. CREWE NECK GATEHOUSE
Rent-a-cop coop.

4. BRITTANY'S HOUSE
Look for the pillars out front. Don't bother looking for a Jacuzzi inside.

5. SATELLITE DISH
Kevin bait: pulls in the Pigskin Channel.

6. UNSTABLE LANDFILL

7. HOME OF TOWN DIRECTOR OF PUBLIC WORKS
1994: Gazebo consumed by sinkhole.

8. CRANBERRY COMMONS
Home of Cashman's, J.J. Jeeters, and Yogurts of the World. Colonial charm, credit-card debt.

9. ADDITIONAL PARKING FOR CRANBERRY COMMONS

10. LAWNDALE HIGH SCHOOL
America's future. Do not feed.

11. TOMMY SHERIDAN MEMORIAL GOALPOST
Site of freak accident that caused the student body to brood for a few days.

12. MORGENDORFFER HOME BASE

13. LANE HOMESTEAD AND MYSTIK SPIRAL MAIL DROP

14. MRS. LANE'S UNDERGROUND CERAMIC BUNKER
Beware of temperamental kiln.

15. LAWNDALE SHOPPING DISTRICT
Where residents do the five percent of their shopping that they don't do at area malls.

16. FORMER SITE OF CAFE LAWNDALE YOUNG ADULT COFFEEHOUSE AND ALT.LAWNDALE.COM CYBERCAFE
Coming soon: Overpriced Seattle Coffee.

You are now entering Lawndale: IQ limits strictly enforced.

A great place to live, work, or live and work in a properly zoned work/living area.

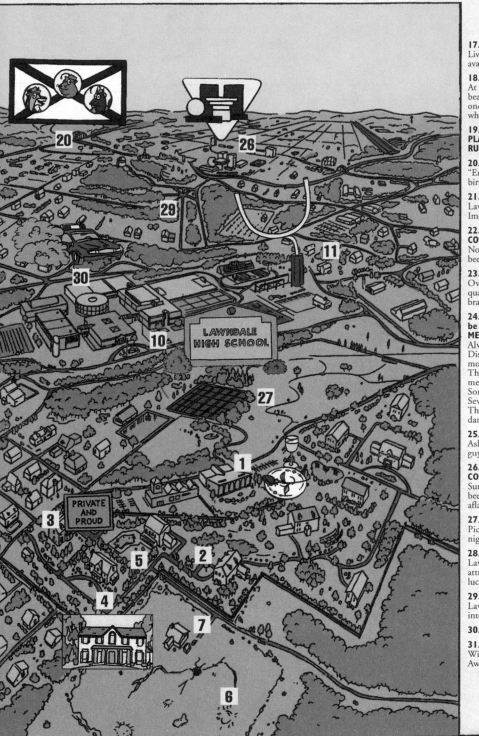

LAWNDALE HIGH SCHOOL

PRIVATE AND PROUD

17. MCGRUNDY'S BREW PUB
Live music nightly. Beer goggles available for a nominal charge.

18. VILLAGE GREEN
At its center, a statue of some bearded guy who was famous once, but no one remembers why.

19. MAN WHO STANDS IN ONE PLACE ALL DAY BOUNCING A RUBBER BALL

20. PIZZA FOREST
"Embarrassing people on their birthdays our specialty."

21. Rx PLEX
Lawndale's One-Stop Body-Image Remake Center.

22. SEDIMENTARY ROCK COUNTRY CLUB AND LINKS
Not restricted. At least no one's been able to prove it in court.

23. LOVERS' LANE
Overlooking the abandoned quarry. Warning: Engage parking brakes before making moves.

24. MULTIMOVIEPLEX (not to be confused with MEGAMULTIPLEX)
Always Playing: Theater 1: Disaster movie; Theater 2: Buddy movie; Theater 3: Chick flick; Theater 4: Former-*SNL*-cast-member vehicle; Theater 5: Something scary; Theater 6: Seventies TV-show remake; Theater 7: Singing animals and dancing teapots.

25. CAR DEALERSHIP STRIP
Ask about our famous "good guy/bad guy" routine.

26. HALCYON HILLS CORPORATE PARK
Sun reflected off buildings has been known to set nearby woods aflame.

27. HIGH HILLS PARK
Picnic tables, tennis courts, nightly Satan worship.

28. THE BIG STRAWBERRY
Lawndale's only roadside attraction. Kiss the stalk for good luck.

29. SEVEN CORNERS
Lawndale's most confusing intersection.

30. SPEED TRAP

31. GUPTY HOUSE
Winner of Town Cute-ification Award.

Lawndale Girls

Daria Morgendorffer
Born alienated.
The world is my
oyster...but I can't
seem to get it open.
Motto: Smart is not a four-letter
word. That would be *smar*.

Jane Lane
Artiste extraordinaire
and pizza fiend. Believes
paint-by-number kits
are inherently evil.
Motto: Every cloud has a
smoky gray lining.

Jodie Landon
Mack's steady date.
Does everything by the
book and returns it to
the library on time.
Motto: Did you order your class
ring yet?

Brittany Taylor
Kevin's main squeeze.
Sugar and spice and
Cosmo advice.
Motto: Rain, rain, go away,
come again another day.
I just did my *hair*!

Quinn Morgendorffer
How lucky can I get—to have such an attractive and popular younger sister? Pass the drain cleaner, please.
Motto: So many dates, so little time. Would you get me a soda?

The Fashion Club How to tell them apart

Tiffany	Purse on her shoulder. Little on her mind.
Sandi	Her voice is deep. Her thoughts are not.
Stacy	Shows her navel. Says nothing novel.

Lawndale girls do a lot of supportive, proactive bonding....well, they get their teeth bonded, anyway.

Daria and Jane Present
The Baby-sitter's New Endings for Classic

PETER PETER PUMPKIN EATER

...Mrs. Eater, while confined to her pumpkin shell, decided to take advantage of this uninterrupted stretch of solitude. She wrote eloquently of her plight. Soon a famous novelist took an interest in her work, campaigned for her release, and had Peter's nose broken by an acquaintance. The resulting book, <u>No Man Can Squash My Spirit!</u>, made the best-seller list, and she eventually got to host her own show on Court TV.

THE EMPEROR'S NEW CLOTHES

...then a little boy cried, "The Emperor is not wearing any clothes!" The crowd gasped. The Emperor was shaken for a moment, but replied, "Of course I'm naked—it's a conceptual art piece about the transparent nature of reality." And since he WAS the Emperor, and had all the money in the kingdom, everyone agreed that it was a very brilliant work and that their leader was in excellent shape for a man of his age. They rejoiced. And a wordy and dense analysis of the event was published in a glossy international art journal and got its editor a juicy curatorship in New York. He was subsequently arrested for wearing the Emperor's new clothes to a reception at a prestigious preparatory school for boys.

ART THOUGHT

Negation and Nakedness

MARY HAD A LITTLE LAMB

...a few weeks passed. One evening, Mary's parents got a call from a caseworker at Lamb Protective Services. "We are bound by state law to make this call investigating signs of possible neglect. One of the teachers at school informs us that your lamb's fleece is no longer white as snow. Also, it seems easily distracted and refuses to change for gym." This was all to Mary's advantage, because her parents were so caught up with the lamb's problems that they didn't even notice that she had been slowly stealing all the silverware in the house.

Guide to Bedtime Stories

THE THREE LITTLE PIGS

...all three pigs moved into the remaining brick house. One day, there was a knock at the door. There was the wolf, who had tired of his thankless role as

reviled pig-eater and had instead decided to capitalize on media-fed paranoia by becoming a door-to-door security system salesman. "In today's dangerous and troubled world, don't you think a security system is an investment you can't afford NOT to make?" Despite the double negative, the pigs agreed, and an elaborate monitoring device was installed. And as long as they kept up the hefty monthly payments, they were never bothered by huffing and puffing again.

THE PRINCESS AND THE PEA

...the old queen placed a pea under a stack of twenty mattresses and said to the princess, "This is for you. It is the most comfortable bed in the kingdom." Unable to sleep, the princess got up to go to the bathroom in the middle of the night and, in her groggy state, forgot to use the ladder. But fate took a hand, and she fell in love with her physical therapist. They collected a healthy settlement on the prince's homeowner's policy and, despite her slight limp, they lived happily ever after.

THE UGLY DUCKLING

...the ugly duckling looked down into the water, and there he beheld a beautiful swan. "Wow!" he thought. "If I can change my life, anyone can." He developed a series of self-improvement tapes and grooming products that he marketed to unattractive animals with poor social skills. He successfully exploited their insecurities, accumulating a large nest egg for himself, and eventually retired to his own private pond with his striking swan trophy wife.

PROTECTED BY GUS LUPUS HOME SECURITY SYSTEMS

Lawndale Guys

Jesse Moreno
Trent's best friend. Plays rhythm guitar in Mystik Spiral. Pet peeves: Top 40 radio, shirts.
Motto: Practice makes perfect. And leather pants don't hurt.

Trent Lane
Jane's older brother. Musician and philosopher. His philosophy involves not making any sudden movements...or gradual ones.
Motto: Be all that you can be. Or at least try and get up before noon.

Charles Ruttheimer III ("Upchuck")
Would be the love child of James Bond and Jerry Lewis, were such a thing possible.
Motto: I like my women like my martinis—shaken *and* stirred. *Rowrr!*

Kevin Thompson
Brittany's half-baked love muffin. He's the BMOC. Too bad he has no idea what it stands for.
Motto: *I* before *E*...except when it's after it, I guess.

Michael Jordan MacKenzie ("Mack")
Jodie's boyfriend and captain of the football team. Has to tolerate Kevin, who has taken a few too many hits to the head.
Motto: He ain't heavy...and he's not my brother, either.

The Three J's — How to tell them apart

Joey	The guy with dark tresses, whom Quinn sure impresses.
Jeffy	The one with red locks, who thinks Quinn's a fox.
Jamie	(aka Jeremy, Jimmy, Jamiel) The one with light hair, who loves Quinn so fair.

It's a man's world, especially when it comes to competitive belching.

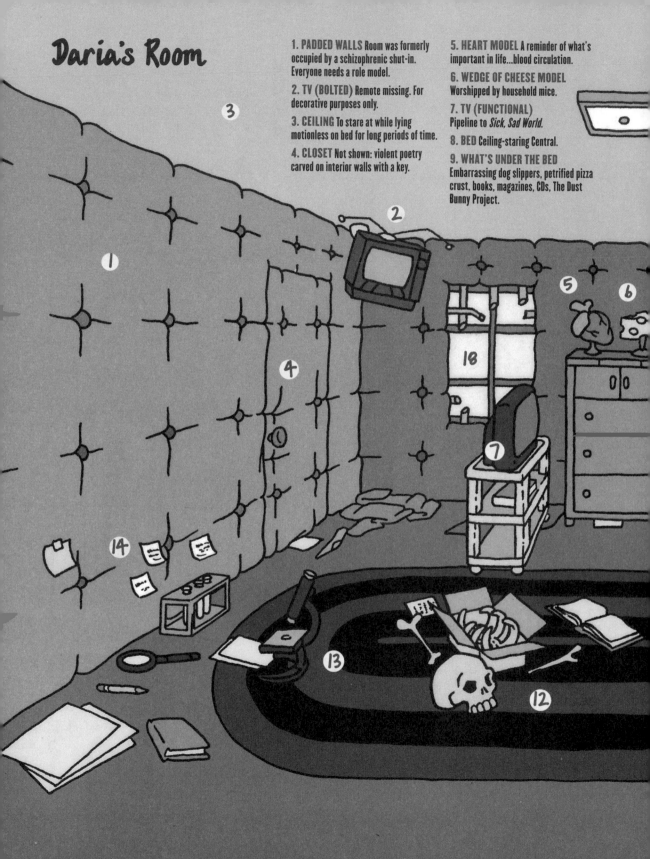

Daria's Room

1. **PADDED WALLS** Room was formerly occupied by a schizophrenic shut-in. Everyone needs a role model.

2. **TV (BOLTED)** Remote missing. For decorative purposes only.

3. **CEILING** To stare at while lying motionless on bed for long periods of time.

4. **CLOSET** Not shown: violent poetry carved on interior walls with a key.

5. **HEART MODEL** A reminder of what's important in life...blood circulation.

6. **WEDGE OF CHEESE MODEL** Worshipped by household mice.

7. **TV (FUNCTIONAL)** Pipeline to *Sick, Sad World*.

8. **BED** Ceiling-staring Central.

9. **WHAT'S UNDER THE BED** Embarrassing dog slippers, petrified pizza crust, books, magazines, CDs, The Dust Bunny Project.

Struck Dumb:
The Love Letters of Kevin and Brittany

LAWNDALE LIONS

DEAR BRITTANY,
I SAW YOU AT CHEER-LEADING TRYOUTS TODAY. I THOUGHT IT WAS REALLY COOL THE WAY YOU SPLIT. (I DON'T MEAN WHEN YOU LEFT, I MEAN WHEN YOU DID A SPLIT.) MY NAME IS KEVIN THOMPSON. I'M ONE OF THOSE GUYS WHO USED TO PEEK THROUGH THE LITTLE WINDOW IN THE GYM DOOR UNTIL THE GYM LADY TAPED A PIECE OF CARDBOARD OVER IT. I'M THE QB ON THE FOOTBALL TEAM—THAT MEANS QUARTERBACK. WILL YOU GO OUT WITH ME? I HAVE A CAR. AND I'M THE QB.

SEE YA!

KEVIN
(THOMPSON)
(QB)

PS: I HOPE THIS IS THE RIGHT LOCKER. IT SMELLS LIKE BABY POWDER.

Brittany's "PAD"

Dear Kevin,
Are you the cute one with the nice teeth who was yelling "Woo-woo!"? You won't believe this, but I asked my friend Jodie about you. She said she heard you were "thick," and I said "I LIKE guys with muscles!" I would love to go out with you. Maybe we can see that cute new Julia Roberts movie!!! I'll meet you after practice. I'll be the one carrying the pom-poms! I gotta go now and tell the other girls to leave their pom-poms in the changing room so you don't get mixed up!!! Can't wait!

Brittany

P.S. That WAS my locker! I could tell this one is yours because of the cleat marks in front of it.

LAWNDALE LIONS

DEAR BRITTANY,
THANKS FOR THE DATE THE OTHER NIGHT. SORRY ABOUT THE MOVIE—I DIDN'T KNOW IT WAS GOING TO BE SO BLOODY. THAT WASN'T THE GUY'S HEAD ANYWAY. NEXT TIME, I SWEAR, YOU GET TO PICK. I THINK WE HAVE A LOT IN COMMON—I CAN'T BELIEVE YOU LIKE JIM CARREY AND FRENCH FRIES TOO! IT'S LIKE MEANINGFUL OR SOMETHING. I GUESS I'LL SEE YOU AT THE GAME. GOOD LUCK WITH THE PYRAMID FORMATION. DON'T LOOK DOWN!

LATER,
KEVIN

Brittany's "PAD"

Dear Kevin,
I had a super time on our date!!! I didn't even mind the yucky "getting chopped up" scene since I couldn't see most of the screen anyway with your face in the way. You were really nice to show me that cool road that looks over the quarry—too bad we couldn't see the rocks in the dark. And I'm glad you were finally able to start your car again. I love the red jeep—there's so much room in the backseat. I mean, compared to one of those little sports thingies. I mean, so I've heard. Anyway, the automatic CD player is very convenient.

Love,
Brittany

Brittany's "PAD"

Dear Kevin,

You could NOT imagine how shocked I was when I walked into that party the other night and saw you with Heidi from the field hockey team. Don't you know that girls who actually PLAY sports instead of CHEERING for GUYS who play sports are bad news with a capital T! Don't expect me to sit back and be some kind of wilted lover. I'm giving you back your ring — maybe your new girlfriend, Heidi, would like to wear it around her big, fat, muscley neck!

Yours Truly,

Brittany

P.S: And why didn't you tell me that those weren't your real shoulders — that they were padding or something? I would have told YOU!!! (Although you KNOW I have nothing to hide — just remember THAT when all you have left are the memories!)

DEAR BRITTANY,

BABE, IT'S NOT WHAT YOU THINK! WE WERE JUST SWAPPING WEIGHT TRAINING TIPS. SHE WAS TELLING ME ABOUT PASSIVE RESISTANCE AND SHE GRABBED MY ARM! YOU KNOW I WOULD NEVER DATE A GIRL WHO IS BIGGER THAN ME. YOU'RE THE ONLY ONE. UNLESS WE BREAK UP, AND THEN I'D HAVE TO FORCE MYSELF TO LOOK AROUND. THE SPORTS BANQUET IS COMING UP AND IT WOULD MEAN A LOT TO HAVE YOU THERE BY MY SIDE. PLUS IF YOU'RE NOT GOING TO GO WITH ME, THEN I DON'T HAVE MUCH TIME TO FIND SOMEBODY ELSE. SO PLEASE BE MY DATE! JUST MEET ME, OK?

LOVE,

KEVIN

Brittany's "PAD"

Dear Kevin,

Well, maybe I COULD forgive you, but it would take an awful lot of sincere caring from you to me. Maybe if you were really, really nice and drove me to the Teddy Bears Collectibles Show at the Coliseum this weekend, and then we could go anklet shopping on the way back.

~~Love~~ Sincerely,

Brittany

DEAR BRITTANY,

I'M GLAD WE MADE UP AND I HOPE YOU LIKE THIS ANKLE BRACELET I BOUGHT FOR YOU WHEN YOU WEREN'T LOOKING THE OTHER DAY AT THE MALL. (I LEFT THE RECEIPT IN THE BOX LIKE YOU SAID TO.) CAN WE DOUBLE-DATE WITH MACK AND JODIE AGAIN? I TOLD THEM THAT WE WANT TO DO SOMETHING FUN LIKE GO TO A WATER PARK — NOT SOMETHING FANCY LIKE THE LAST TIME WHEN WE WENT TO THAT BORING VIOLIN CONCERT AND THE RESTAURANT THAT DIDN'T HAVE BREAD STICKS.

LOVE,

KEVIN

Brittany's "PAD"

Dear Kevin,
  It's our five-and-a-half-month anniversary and I am super-happy to be with you. I know we've had our ups and downs, but you've always come through for me—even when it meant you had to borrow your Dad's credit card. And I know I've come through for you—even when I've been really pooped. We have so much to look forward to in the future. I can just picture us growing old together—I bet we'll still be cute!
  (Or at least cuter than all the other old people!!!)

      Kisses and Hugs!!!
              Brittany

LAWNDALE LIONS

DEAR BRITTANY,
  SORRY I FORGOT THE FIVE-AND-A-HALF-MONTH ANNIVERSARY, BUT I THOUGHT WE WERE DOING EVERY 30 DAYS. IF YOU WRITE UP A SKEDULE SCHEDULE FOR ME, THEN I WON'T MISS ANY MORE. I DON'T WANT TO MAKE YOU MAD AGAIN. I REALLY LIKE HAVING A HOT GIRLFRIEND LIKE YOU—IT MAKES ALL THE OTHER GUYS JEALOUS! AND YOU ARE COOL IN OTHER WAYS TOO: I'M ALWAYS SURPRISED AT HOW FAR YOUR VOICE CARRIES ON THE FIELD!

      LOVE,
      KEVIN

Brittany's "PAD"

Dear Kevin,
  Are you saying I'm a basic sex object? Sometimes I think you can't see my brains at all! I am more than just a plaything! I am a sensitive person with feelings and thoughts who listens to sad music when I'm bummed out and reads magazines and sometimes even books.
  Watch it!
              Brittany

LAWNDALE LIONS

DEAR BRITTANY,
  YOU GOT IT ALL WRONG AGAIN! I THINK YOU ARE PERFECT THE WAY YOU ARE. AND YOUR BRAINS ARE AWESOME. YOU KNOW, I THINK WE SHOULD STOP WITH THE NOTES. LET'S JUST TALK IN PERSON. WHEN I WRITE STUFF DOWN, IT COMES OUT ALL STUPID. AND WE DON'T GET TO DO THE THINGS THAT MAKE US WANT TO KEEP GOING OUT.
      KEV

Dear Kevin,
  Well all right then.
See you under the bleachers.
              Brit

CREATIVE WRITING: MR. O'NEILL

Due 3/20

This week's assignment is to write a short story in which your main character overcomes adversity and learns a valuable lesson. Remember: To receive a passing grade, you must utilize both simile AND metaphor. Don't forget to use your imagination! And although this is a short story, I expect at least 100 words.

I WOKE UP IN THE FUTURE!!!
by Charles Ruttheimer III

I woke up seeing stars.

My head was spinning like a Vegas roulette wheel on New Year's Eve. Where was I? My eyes focused upon a quartet of beautiful aliens, busy massaging my feet and hands. They would have been indistinguishable from the more desirable type of female *Homo sapien* if not for their pointed claws, unusually curvaceous figures, and thigh-high boots made of an unidentifiable ultrashiny substance. *Excellent use of descriptive language!*

It seemed like just yesterday that I had stepped into my experimental time-travel module and shut the door on my former life. I, Jack Hardison, inventor and man of action.

I soon realized that the most hypnotically fetching alien was speaking English. Could this be...could I be...on Earth???

"You see, all the males on your planet killed each other long ago," explained the attractive Amazon with the huge green eyes like almonds—if almonds were white and had big black dots in the middle of them. She told me her name, but I could not pronounce it, as I had bitten my human tongue in surprise. "We colonized the globe and taught your women to clone themselves and perfect their physical beauty. Now that they are self-sufficient, our job is done. We were about to return to our home planet, but when you arrived in your time-traveling spaceship, we realized that this was our one opportunity to observe the strange creature called 'man' that we had heard so much about."

So I was the lone male on a planet of females. A stray eel among angelfish. A single potato chip in a bowl of pretzels. What a grave responsibility.

They lifted me up upon their shoulders, which were strong yet supple, and carried me off. I rode a wave of fleshy loveliness

Quinn's Room

1. **MAKEUP CENTRAL** The Temple of Groom.

2. **POM-POM** Quinn was going to try out for cheerleading, until she realized everyone has to wear the same outfit.

3. **TRUNK** Maybe Quinn will climb into it someday and disappear.

4. **STUFFED DOG** A gift from Jamie. She told Jeffy and Joey it was a birthday present from Grandma Morgendorffer.

5. **BULLETIN BOARD** To help keep track of all her activities...so she can decide which ones to blow off first.

6. **MIRRORS** Can't have too many of these! Though Quinn tries.

7. **WINDOW** At night, Quinn looks up at the vast heavens and thinks seriously about what shoes to wear.

8. **JEWELRY BOX** All that glitters is not gold. Especially when you buy it at J.J Jeeters.

9. **STUFFED DINO** Joey gave it to her. Told Jeffy and Jamie she won it playing Skee-Ball.

10. **SMILEY FACE PILLOW** Smile plastered on its face. Full of fluff. Resemble anyone?

Quinn has a dream room. Caused by eating too much cotton candy before bedtime.

11. CANOPY BED Fit for a princess. The kind who falls into a deep sleep that lasts for hundreds of years. I can dream, can't I?

12. STUFFED DUCK Jeffy gave it to her. She ran out of stories so she had to come clean. Now Joey, Jeffy, and Jamie are chipping in for a six-foot-tall plush giraffe.

13. GLASSES For reading. Who left *those* here?

14. BUBBLE GUM MACHINE Emptying out gradually...like Quinn's head.

15. POSTERS OF BOY BABES Quinn wishes real guys could learn to keep this quiet.

16. WHAT'S UNDER THE BED Miscellaneous anklets, hairballs, scrunchies, hairbrushes, clothes, socks, and half-written letter to Peruvian pen pal.

17. CARPETING So the sound of foot-stamping won't disturb those below.

Lack of Faculty: The Teachers of Lawndale High

Ms. Claire Defoe
Art
Jewelry as large as her imagination. Resents being forced to choose between "arts" and "crafts."

Ms. Janet Barch
Science
Hypothesis: Bitter divorce results in intense resentment of all males. Of any species.

Mr. Anthony DeMartino
History
Thinks teachers' editions are for wimps. Beneath his gruff exterior, he's a puppy dog. A rabid puppy dog.

Mrs. Diane Bennett
Economics
Lives for the clicky-clack sound that chalk makes. Her confusing diagrams are legendary, as is her hatred of pennies.

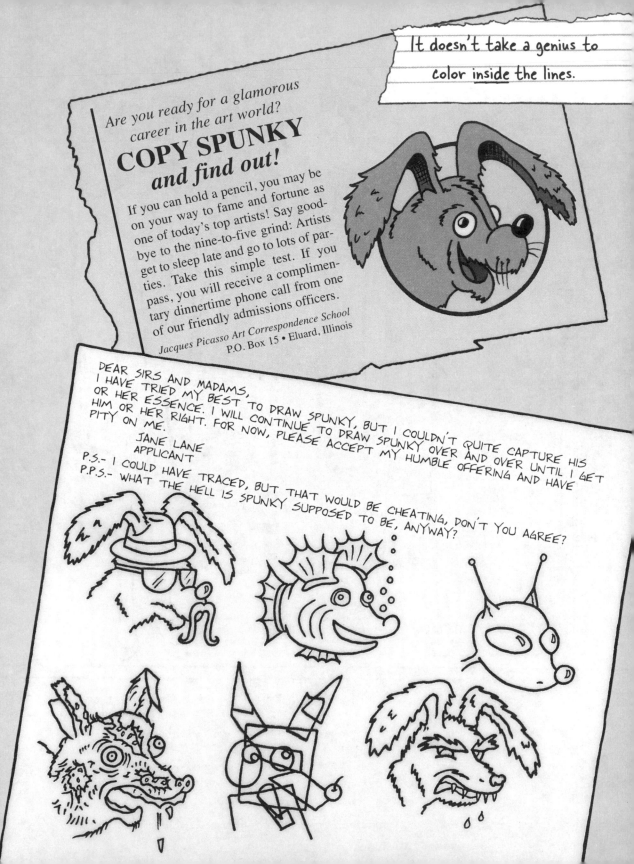

Started school this week. It's reassuring to know that no matter where you go, kids are the same...stupid and shallow. Shockingly, Quinn fit in immediately; now she's managed to convince her new friends that it's just a coincidence that two girls named Morgendorffer happened to start school on the same day. I kind of admire her for that. The way you'd admire Attila the Hun for being focused.

Not everyone here is friendly and popular. There's this one girl named Jane who is snide, antisocial, and resentful. Finally, a friend. Jane invited me over after school to watch Sick, Sad World and help barricade the front door in case someone tried to foreclose on the house. (Her parents are out of the country for a few months and forgot to leave the mortgage payments.) I met her brother, Trent. He's a musician, which means he sleeps all day and doesn't have a job. This is a cool family.

Trent started talking to me, and the conversation was going pretty well until he fell asleep. Jane says that's his worst habit, and that it's really annoying when he does it while driving. But Trent asleep is more interesting than Quinn awake.

Hmm, maybe I'd better burn this page. I'd hate for this diary to come back to haunt me when I'm nominated to the Supreme Court.

Masochist's
~~Magical~~ Memories

I refuse to say "cheese" unless it is followed by "burger."

Let me guess. It squeaks.

Who are you people, and what do you want from me?

Quinn takes her first baby steps. Too bad she didn't keep going.

Quinn never showed up.
She couldn't decide on an outfit.

The teacup ride was where things really got out of hand.

Quinn in her awkward stage.
It lasted about a week.

The Grand Canyon.
Mom was really
impressed.

I always got invited to slumber parties. I was
the only one with an adult library card.

I told the counselor that I
couldn't participate in Color War
because it was against my religion.
And that kickboards were the
work of the Devil.

On our way to my cousin's wedding. Hello, 911?

Quinn has a thing for men in uniform.

A new chapter begins.
Too bad it's the same old book.

LAWNDALE LIONS

TO: ALL TEAM MEMBERS

FROM: MICHAEL JORDAN MACKENZIE, CAPTAIN

PAIN IS PASSING. PRIDE IS PERMANENT.

LET'S TACKLE BUS BEHAVIOR

This is your wake-up call, guys. Some changes need to be made around here. The discipline and sportsmanship we display on the field is not evident on the bus. We shouldn't fumble our hard-won reputation for excellence: Let's be known for our triple-threat ground attack, not for tying the entire Oakwood marching band together with elastic bandages.

I'm sure our coach, Mr. Gibson, would agree. (Update: He's almost done paying his debt to society and assures me that when the recruiter used the word "kickback," Mr. Gibson thought he said "kick<u>off</u>.")

Please read this handout more than once, so the rules stick in your brain.

THE FOLLOWING PRACTICES ARE FORBIDDEN:

1. Hiding cheerleaders in the little bathroom at the back of the bus.
2. Punting helmets in the aisle.
3. Forcing any teammate to wear his wristband as a belt.
4. Carbo-loading someone against his will.
5. Using your head as a weapon (off the field).
6. Throwing protective cups out the windows—they're not cheap, you know.
7. Pouring sports drink over the driver's head while the bus is in motion.
8. Stuffing the towel boy into the overhead rack.
9. Hanging out the windows and picking fights with tractor-trailer drivers.
10. Singing the fight song more than ten times in a row. (Sure it's catchy, but let's save those vocal cords for the game. Humming is equally annoying—especially if you are the quarterback and have been told a hundred times.)

MACK

Due 3/20
This week's assignment is to write a short story in which your main

OUR SPARKLY LOVE
By Brittany Taylor

Chelsea Talbot was the most successful woman in the world of making hats. She lived a fancy life that most people only have dreams about. She could get champagne anytime and had a really big house, which was also tastefully decorated. But something was missing. Could it be...love?

She was born poor and not pretty. Her real name was Gertrude, but she changed it. She knew she had to become a different person if she was going to escape from the farm in Nebraska and end up rich and famous, so she saved up her allowance and went to Paris where she learned French and how to dress nice and dyed her hair red. Now she was a fox!

You lost an opportunity here to elaborate on the fox metaphor.

There was a knock at her office door. She combed her fingers through her fiery mane and then got up to answer it.

"Hello, Chelsea."

It was Rake Bohan—her rival and archenemy. He had a pouty mouth and black wavy hair and a body like a sculpture, but he was snotty. Still...what was he really like underneath the lousy exterior?

"I came for the money. And you better give it to me or I'll go to the newspapers and tell them all about your affair with the Duke of Tahiti."

His lower lip curled in a cruel way. He knew the Duke of Tahiti was married and the news would cause quite a scandal. (By the way, she was an innocent virgin at the time and didn't even know there was a Duchess!)

All of a sudden, she remembered her night with the Duke of Tahiti—she in her piece of cloth that wraps around the waist and he in his thing like a bathrobe, but without the belt. She thought it was love then, but it was probably more of a fling. No, she had never been in love. Not yet.

"What do you want? Money?"

Rake smiled. It was an evil smile, but cute.

"No, I HAVE money. I want YOU."

Well-integrated simile!

The air in the room all of a sudden got like a sauna. But Chelsea couldn't open up the windows, since it was an office building with the kind of windows you can't open.

She remembered when she had first laid eyes on Rake. She had just dove off a cliff in the South of France and as a big white boat happened to

Daria and Jane's
All-Time Favorite Episodes of
SICK, SAD WORLD

1. SECRET SCOUT SCANDALS
These tough cookies are a disgrace to the uniform. A brutalized troop leader speaks out.

2. PSYCHIC CENTERFOLDS
What happens when Miss September can see November? She's a triple D with ESP!

3. "I'M MY OWN GRANDPA"
His father married his stepdaughter. But look out—here comes a bouncing baby boy!

4. TOP NUN
Meet the Jewish Marine drill sergeant who entered a convent after his/her sex change. Talk about converting!

5. "HELP! MY SIAMESE TWIN DRESSES TOO SEXY!"
They share one body—and *what* a body! But can our makeover team please them both?

6. "OUR MOM'S A BITCH!"
Separated at birth and sent to live with strangers, puppy sibs are reunited at last. Now they have a bone to pick with Mom.

7. NUDE BOOK CLUBS
Is it about brains or bods? A revealing look at a controversial social phenomenon that's really taking off.

8. WHEN ALIENS CAN'T COMMIT
Contactees fed up with their flighty alien beaus. Plus: A certified therapist's advice on how to land your man, woman, or whatever it is.

Schrecter, Eric

From: Morgendorffer, Helen
To: Schrecter, Eric
Subject: Sleepy surgeon

Priority: High

Mrs. Garcia wants to settle. I think litigation would be a big mistake: Dr. Krakow has admitted to me that he fell asleep briefly during the operation and was temporarily "all turned around" upon awakening. An entire team of residents viewed the procedure, so I believe that our original claim that a preexisting skin condition caused the partial removal of a perfectly healthy spleen won't hold water. And I want these photos off my desk! Two hundred thou and let's all get on with our lives.

Schrecter, Eric

1

From: Morgendorffer, Helen
To: Schrecter, Eric
Subject: Rethinking Dress-Down Friday

Priority: Medium

As you usually take off early on summer weekends (how's the beach house, by the way?), I thought you should be informed of recent developments regarding the implementation of Dress-Down Friday. The program has gotten out of hand, Eric: I just saw one of the first-year associates sporting flip-flops and cutoffs, and the third floor paralegals are apparently under the impression that they're on the Olympic swim team. Let's get a handle on this problem before we have complete wardrobe chaos and more sexual harassment suits to deal with. (Let me state—on the record—that I'm not saying wearing a white halter top and shorty shorts is **any** sort of invitation to **anything**.)

Schrecter, Eric

1

From: Morgendorffer, Helen
To: Schrecter, Eric
Subject: Hinge Expert Hightails It

Priority: Urgent

Our expert witness in the Peterson door-hinge liability case has backed out. He claims to have gotten a "better gig" with the collapsed-lifeguard-chair proceedings that have everyone talking. We must address this problem immediately: We are losing them left and right to high-profile circuses with televised proceedings. Either we up the ante or the only expert witness we'll have left is the guy from the newsstand downstairs who knows a whole lot about gum.

Schrecter, Eric

1

From: Morgendorffer, Helen
To: Schrecter, Eric
Subject: Next Wednesday

Priority: High

Just wanted to give you fair warning that I will be out of the office from 3:00 to 3:20 next Wednesday. I will be reachable by phone, of course. You have the number.

Schrecter, Eric

1

From: Morgendorffer, Helen
To: Schrecter, Eric
Subject: An update

Priority: High

The in-house counsel of Concepts in Construction remains uncooperative. They have changed their strategy five times in the last five days. Their latest harebrained scheme is to claim that collapsed scaffolding is an Act of God. Where do we get these clients, anyway? And the animal rights people are marching out front again. (BTW, what's the status of the lap-dancing cat case?) Who needs this mishegoss? I should have gone into maritime law.

Schrecter, Eric

1

From: Morgendorffer, Helen
To: Schrecter, Eric
Subject: Better to bow out...

Priority: High

I'm afraid that I must excuse myself from the defective-scrunchie class-action suit due to a conflict of interest. I have just discovered that the individual whose initial complaint instigated the proceedings is my daughter Quinn. (Believe me, I am not happy about this—I could use the billable hours.)

I like musicians. They make me look motivated.

McGrundy's PUB

18 Main Street • Lawndale
Live and Recorded Music Seven Nights a Week
Try our Shovel Full O' Onion Rings!

COMING UP:

FRIDAY
Ted O'Shaunessy
and his Songs of Starvation

SATURDAY
Sons of Morris
A Tribute to the Doors

SUNDAY
Mystik Spiral
Introspective Rock and Roll

MONDAY
Jagger Meister
Sounds of the Stones

TUESDAY
Motown Dance Party (with DJ Jimmy Jumps)
Women drink tropical drinks free before 10

WEDNESDAY
Opal
Plaintive longings

THURSDAY
Showcase Night
Open mike. Take your chances.

You must be over 21 to drink.
No lame fake IDs, please—we've seen them all.

PLUSH RECORDS
45 RPM

MYSTIK SPIRAL
SIDE A
"BEHIND MY EYELIDS"
(LANE/MORENO)

MYSTIK SPIRAL

BEHIND MY EYELIDS

R.I.P.

B/W
ICEBOX
WOMAN

MUCK & RAGE

The purest 'zine on the indie scene

SHOW REVIEWS

Mystik Spiral
McGrundy's Brew Pub
April 16

reviewed by Mike Z.

Guitar and Vocals: Trent Lane
Rhythm Guitar: Jesse Moreno
Bass: Nicholas Campbell
Drums: Max Tyler

When I arrived at McGrundy's, already in a foul mood because this jerk in a Camaro cut me off and stole my parking space, my name wasn't even on the list. And then this arty chick at the bar wouldn't talk to me, acting like she was the queen of something. I only showed up because I heard the bass player used to play with Iggy, but they must have played Monopoly—because he sucked! The singer was this skinny guy who was just the type my ex-girlfriend would think is cute—some moody pretty boy with a stupid tribal tattoo. The music was about as exciting as a house-plant. The drummer sure can sweat, though. The bartender was stingy with the shots and gave me this dirty look when I lit up my cigar. (I know what you're thinking, but I was smoking them way back before the whole trend started, and I wouldn't be caught dead in some asinine cigar bar.) I kept thinking about my ex and these sickening phonies she's hanging around with

---

PRESSED IN
THE U.S.
VINYL LIVES!

SMUDGE MAGAZINE
Record Reviews

MYSTIK SPIRAL
"Behind My Eyelids" / "Icebox Woman"
Plush Records

This debut release from Mystik Spiral, a convincingly tormented quartet, is chock-full of impassioned playing and suburban angst. Trent Lane's dark brand of moody self-absorption should appeal to fans of Sisters of Mercy, Bauhaus, rainy days, black eyeliner, and decadent French Romantic poets. Rhythm guitarist Jesse Moreno, formerly of the goth/synth group Bats With Guns ("Baby Shakes Her Death Rattle"), contributes a distinctive chunka-chunk texture. "Behind My Eyelids" is a forlorn ballad that packs a mother lode of image-laden fantasy. Although lines like "As lashes close, I see my woes, spread out like a carpet of bugs" verge on self-parody, the band's emotional intensity won me over. "Icebox Woman," on the other hand, which mines the familiar territory of obsessive love, is innovative only in its use of humming. It sounds like it was recorded in a wind tunnel, which works to its advantage, yet

Upchuck Central

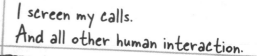

(CLICK) This is Charles. I can't come to the phone right now, because I am occupado. I could tell you what I am doing, but let's not ruin the mystery. At the tone, leave your name, number, and the time you called, and I will get back to you as soon as I can tear myself away from my life of intrigue, about which I cannot be specific, lest I put both my life and yours in danger. (BEEP)

(CLICK) No, no...not now, girls! This is Charles Ruttheimer the Third, and you have reached my answering machine...please, ladies, patience!...speak clearly at the tone and...I'm on my way, my dears!...they *so* hate to be kept waiting...anyway, I'll get back to you as soon as possible...if this is an emergency, well, so is a woman on fire! (BEEP)

(CLICK) You have successfully contacted the underground grotto of The Ruttheimer Group, currently engineering our secret plan to achieve world domination by the year 2010. If you would like to know more about our plans to gain global control of mass media, subjugate the military forces of every nation on Earth, and install Charles Ruttheimer the Third as supreme ruler of all humankind, please leave your name and address at the beep, and we will send you an informative brochure and a free bumper sticker. (BEEP)

(CLICK) This is the answering machine of Charles Ruttheimer the Second. To those business associates who have attempted to call me at home while I was overseas, please accept my apologies for the answering machine messages of the past few days. At the tone, please leave your name, number, and a brief description of what you feel would be an appropriate punishment for my son. (BEEP)

It could have been worse. They could have been married in a hot tub.

Jake and Helen

Vows of Commitment

June 26, 1975

Together Under an open sky and upon sacred ground, I acknowledge the oneness of the universe. May the cosmic forces bless our union and make it a journey of enlightenment.

Helen I pledge my commitment to your growth and self-realization. I respect your beingness. I recognize your personhood. I promise to get out of the way and let you discover who you are. I will not get on your case or nag.

Jake I place this garland on your crown as a symbol of the never-ending circle of life and death—a journey we shall take together. Merging lives is a pretty big deal. I pledge that I have thought this thing out and really want to do it.

Together We will raise our children to be independent spirits, free from oppressive rules and society's expectations—an organic expression of our physical love.

Let us begin this karmic adventure. In the presence of friends and trees, we take each other as man and woman. The revolution begins with us!

Jake Morgendorffer, Capricorn

Helen Barksdale, Cancer

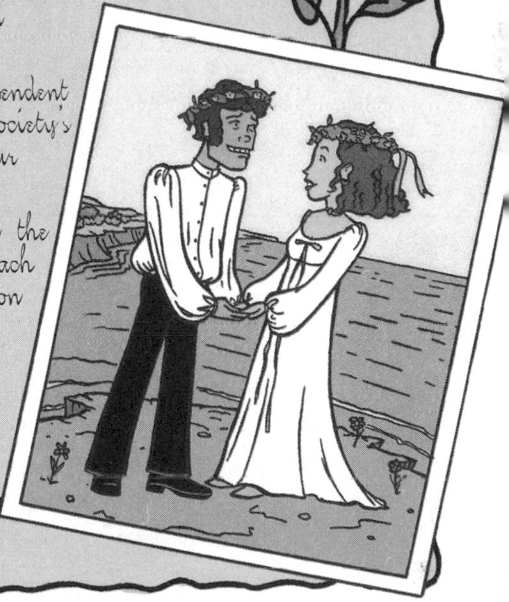

ALTERNAPALOOZA

3 DAYS OF MUSIC, MUD, AND MAYHEM!

24 BANDS. AT LEAST 24 PORTABLE TOILETS.

AUGUST 15,16,17
SWEDESVILLE

Appearing...

SIGOURNEY • CREASE
CIGGIE BUTT

PLUS...THE REMAINING MEMBERS OF FOAM PARTY

Also appearing...

Cute Shiny Things	Spit Take	No Parking Anytime
Angry Toads	Instant Rewind	Loathsome Cowboys
Happenin' Sistahs	Isadora Dunkin'	Mr. Glow and Mr. Worm
My Ass Hurts	Rotten Candy	The Kneeknockers
Pool	Box Storage	First Degree Felony
Flaxen	Lint Factory	Hopatchong
The Elephant Seals	The Nuzzles	

• NIGHTLY MUCKPIT RAVE • ANARCHO-ECO-ACTIVIST AREA •
• CYBERPOETRY SLAM •
• AND THE FAMOUS JACK SPRAT PHOTOGENIC SIDESHOW •
• MUNCHABLES AVAILABLE •
PRICE: $75

(Woodstock's over. Touch the fence and you're toast.)

Printed on hemp: The world's most durable fiber.

HOW TO GET TO THE FEST

My parents want me to live up to my potential, so I'm careful not to let them know what it is.

EDITORIAL

LIVING UP TO YOUR POTENTIAL

By Jodie Landon
Honor Society President

Perfection is a goal we should strive for, although we may never achieve it. It is an ideal we cannot realize, a destination we can never reach—yet all the more compelling because of its unattainable nature. Perfection fuels our accomplishments. It sits upon our horizon; we move forward, yet it recedes as we approach.

Perhaps the lifelong struggle begins in infancy, when one baby is content to settle for her thumb, while another gropes for the brightly colored mobile just out of reach.

But as that striving child matures, she discovers that she can't be all things to all people. If she manages to please Mother by blazing a trail in the corporate world, then how can she fulfill Father's dream of seeing her as a shaper of public policy, stamping the family name upon historic legislation? Besides, what if she really want to be a ballerina?

So what if you *would* rather lie on the grass and look for shapes in the clouds? That's what retirement's for. For now, you have to get into college, then grad school. Pause for a single moment and someone else may take the lead. Fun is a luxury you cannot afford.

Is there any way out? Should you admit that you're not all that superior to the so-called "norm"? Will the admission of a single mistake start an inevitable slide into poverty and disgrace? Do you often feel like you are playing a part and hiding your true self? Are you constantly asking yourself rhetorical questions? And why *are* you dating the captain of the football team—because you like him, or because he's who he is and you're who you are and others don't care to question the equation?

So remember: There can be only one valedictorian, but there is no limit to the number of people who can try to be valedictorian and fail. So whether you are up on that podium on graduation day, or sitting way in the back making fun of me, always do your very best—never mind the terrible, terrible toll it may take on your spirit.

Have a great summer!

THE PINCUS-BIZET SELF-CONCEPT INVENTORY

Dear Student:

Answer the following questions at your own speed and to the best of your ability. This test is practically confidential—the results will be shared with just a few adults who have only your best interests at heart. Have fun!

Mrs. Manson
School Psychologist

Name: *Quinn Morgendorffer*

1a. Is this glass half empty or half full? *Half full*
1b. How does that make you feel? *Like the waiter isn't very good, and he won't be getting much of a tip.*

2. Draw the animal that best represents you in the space below:

3. What does this shape make you think of?
How much it costs to dry-clean silk.

4. As you read each word below, write down the first thing that comes to mind.
    a. black *leggings*
    b. new *for fall*
    c. big *savings*
    d. low *calorie*
    e. up *scale*

5. What is this girl thinking?
How is it possible to combine conditioner and shampoo in one hair-care product?

6. If you could change one thing about yourself, what would it be?
I would tan more evenly.

7. If I disappeared from the face of the earth tomorrow, no one would notice or care. True or false. *Mrs. Manson, I would care! Cheer up!*

8. Other people often don't understand that I....
...look like a size 3, but sometimes have to take a size 5.

9. Is this a bunny or a duck?
A bunny—but not a very cute one.

10. Which item doesn't belong? Why?
D. They don't make corn-flavored gum.

STOP! Do not go on to the next page unless told to do so,
or you may be labeled a delinquent personality.

THE PINCUS-BIZET SELF-CONCEPT

Dear Student:
Answer the following questions at your own speed and to the best of your ability. This test is practically confidential—the results will be shared with just a few adults who have only your best interests at heart. Have fun!

Mrs. Manson
School Psychologist

Name: Daria Morgendorffer

1a. Is this glass half empty or half full? half empty
1b. How does that make you feel? half bored to death

2. Draw the animal that best represents you in the space below:

PIGEON →

← HOLE

3. What does this shape make you think of?
The darkness within. Or maybe it's a butterfly contemplating the darkness within.

4. As you read each word below, write down the first thing that comes to mind.
   a. black future
   b. new strain of Ebola
   c. big pain in the butt
   d. lowest common denominator
   e. up up and away

5. What is this girl thinking?

What happened to my legs?

6. If you could change one thing about yourself, what would it be? My planet.

7. If I disappeared from the face of the earth tomorrow, no one would notice or care. True or false. False. I owe the Mob quite a bit of money.

8. Other people often don't understand that I......will be back someday to get them.

9. Is this a bunny or a duck? Neither. I would consider it a dunny.

10. Which item doesn't belong? Why?

A) B) C) D)

D. It's the only one I'm not planning to throw during the next assembly.

STOP! Do not go on to the next page unless told to do so, or you may be labeled a delinquent personality.

It's far too late to worry about that.

Mr. O'Neill's Memory Boosters

From the desk of TIMOTHY O'NEILL

Optimist's Weekly

NAME GAMES *(continued from page 67)*

TIP THREE: PICTURE THIS!

One way to remember a name is to visualize a unique and arresting image and associate it with the person you have just met. Thus, if you are introduced to a fellow named George, you might think of George Washington, and picture your new acquaintance with a white wig on his head and a large ax in his hand, chopping down a cherry tree. Absurd images work best—but don't get caught giggling! (This creates a poor first impression.)

DAR(I)(A)
rhymes with SARI
"ahhhh!" like when the doctor sticks a tongue depressor in your mouth (eew!)

DARIA

JANE as in JANE Doe, significant other of JOHN Doe → "Doe A Deer" That one was easy!

KEVIN
Rhymes with →HEAVEN and reminds me of KEVIN Costner in "Dances With Wolves"—what an uplifting movie!

JODIE
like JOE DiMAGGIO without the "Maggio"

— Maybe these are getting too complicated

BRITAIN + KNEE = BRITTANY!
Ouch!

MACK → SACK

(MACK)ERAL
↑ overkill?

CHARLES — CHARLES Dickens—my favorite author! wrote "Oliver Twist"
'Please, sir, I want some more!'
Now I'm going to think that red-headed kid's name is Oliver. THIS DOESN'T WORK AT ALL!!!

Due 3/20
This week's assignment is to write a short story in which your main
character overcomes adversity and learns a valuab...

A REALLY COOL STORY ABOUT THIS COUPLE WHO WERE IN A CAR AND HEARD ON THE RADIO ABOUT A GUY WHO ESCAPED FROM THE MENTAL HOSPITAL WITH A HOOK FOR A HAND

By Kevin Thompson

$7+9=16$

$7+9$

$16+16=32+3=35$

$7+5$
7
5

This is a story about someone who overcomes adversity and learns a valuable lesson. It happened to a friend of a friend of mine.

$35+5+5=45$
$7+7=14$ $\begin{array}{r}45\\+14\\\hline 59\end{array}$

(Does the title count? Because if it does, I have 67 words, but if it doesn't I only have 44...I mean, 47.)

$\begin{array}{r}59\\+8\\\hline 67\\+16\\\hline 83\end{array}$ $\begin{array}{r}100\\-83\\\hline 17\end{array}$

It's hard to write a story when you have to keep worrying about how long it is. If you keep counting over and over, how can you concentrate? Like right there, that was 75 words. Make that 94 if you include this sentence but not the title. One more and I'm done! The

10
$+7=17$

Kevin,
see me.

At reception—Ask about Mel's kids, DON'T mention Rod's wife

Eye contact!!!

DRAFT

ON THE FRONT LINES OF TELEMARKETING
Presentation by Jake Morgendorffer
Jake Morgendorffer Consulting, Inc.

Welcome, members of the Marketing Consultants Networking Ring, to this month's Proven Profits Power Breakfast. I'm Jake Morgendorffer. Many of you already know me as the man behind the successful long-term vertically integrated strategy that resulted in the RUMP PUMP's meteoric rise to the top of the ~~exercise gizmo~~ *health-enhancement hardware market* —20 million dollars in sales annually. ~~Others of you perhaps credit that idea-stealing polygamist Mike Patrick.~~ But I'm not here to brag...I'm here to inform.

Smile (sincere)

Finger-sign quote marks for "bad rap"

This morning, I'd like to speak to the topic of telemarketing—an essential outreach tool that's been given a "bad rap" as far as I'm concerned. Offering consumers access to life-changing products (with a 30-day money-back guarantee!) is no crime. Used to strengthen the human bond between supplier and consumer, telemarketing is, at its very worst, *a passing annoyance.* ~~an infuriating intrusion.~~ But at its very best, it is both effective AND legal. ~~And you want to talk about cheap! The words "minimum wage" simply do not exist in~~

But how to overcome consumer resistance to the telemarketer's message? Never forget that foresight in hiring practices is the key to effective sell-through.

sensitive types

The last thing you need is a crew of ~~overgrown babies~~ whose immediate reaction to outright hostility is to succumb to teary-eyed self-pity. Who cares if some perfect stranger just called you a goddamn jerk or blew a whistle into the phone or made an obscene remark implying an unhealthy relationship between yourself and a close relative? ~~Especially if it's true, ha ha!~~ The next number on your list may pay off in the big sale you've been waiting for. You need a thick skin in this ~~demeaning, cutthroat~~ *competitive*

If face twitches, press on temple with index finger.

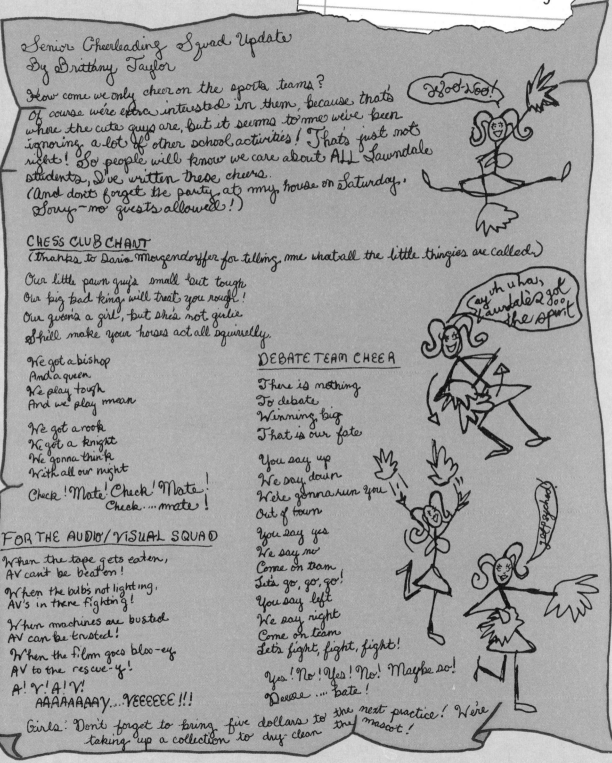

Senior Cheerleading Squad Update
By Brittany Taylor

How come we only cheer on the sports teams?
Of course we're extra interested in them, because that's
where the cute guys are, but it seems to me we've been
ignoring a lot of other school activities! That's just not
right! So people will know we care about ALL Lawndale
students, I've written these cheers.
(And don't forget the party at my house on Saturday.
 Sorry—no guests allowed!)

WOO-WOO!

CHESS CLUB CHANT
(Thanks to Daria Morgendoffer for telling me what all the little thingies are called.)

Our little pawn guy's small but tough
Our big bad king will treat you rough!
Our queen's a girl, but she's not girlie
She'll make your horses act all squirrelly.

We got a bishop
And a queen
We play tough
And we play mean

We got a rook
We got a knight
We gonna think
With all our might

Check! Mate! Check! Mate!
        Check ..... mate!

Say uh uh, Lawndale's got the spirit

DEBATE TEAM CHEER

There is nothing
To debate
Winning big
That is our fate

You say up
We say down
We're gonna run you
Out of town

You say yes
We say no
Come on team
Let's go, go, go!
You say left
We say right
Come on team
Let's fight, fight, fight!

Yes! No! Yes! No! Maybe so!
Deeee ..... bate!

FOR THE AUDIO/VISUAL SQUAD

When the tape gets eaten,
AV can't be beaten!

When the bulb's not lighting,
AV's in there fighting!

When machines are busted
AV can be trusted!

When the film goes bloo-ey
AV to the rescue-y!

A! V! A! V!
    AAAAAAAAY....VEEEEEE!!!

LET'S go Lawndale!

Girls: Don't forget to bring five dollars to the next practice! We're
        taking up a collection to dry-clean the mascot!

Experience the multilevel, climate-controlled thrill of nonstop shopping. Your own personal purchasing paradise awaits!

DIRECTORY

APPAREL
1. The Sports Shorts
2. Wild West Vests
3. Socks by Seth
4. Leather and Lycra
5. Husky Guy Hut
6. The Stork Set
7. Bridal Barn
8. Feetniks
9. L'Impressions
10. Sir Jeff Menswear
11. Patty's Plus-Size Palace
12. Everything's Purple

DEPARTMENT STORES
13. Spackle & Spackle
14. Gish's
15. W.H. Trogg

GIFTS
16. The Doo Dad Shop
17. Have a Cow!
18. Wicks of Wonder
19. Fuzzy Wuzzy Shop
20. Hi-Fi Hi-Fi Hi-Fi
21. Books by the Ton
22. Sound by the Pound
23. Poster Pad
24. The Honey Pot
25. Country Cushions
26. The Cheddary
27. We Are Toys
28. The 99 Cents-and-Up Store

SPECIALTY SHOPS
29. Claw and Paw
30. Beak and Squeak
31. It's Just Vacuum Cleaner Bags
32. Plantamonium
33. The Vapid Koala
34. Jellybean Junction
35. Oh, My Aching Back!
36. Makeup Mill
37. Cuter Computer
38. Drugs 'n' Stuff
39. My Ass Hurts
40. The Cart Mart
41. Bikini Island
42. Sunglasseteria
43. Earring Eave
44. Temporary Tattoo Tower

SERVICES
45. Scizzor Wizzard Unisex Haircutters
46. Fancy Pretty Nail
47. Multiple Memories Photo Studio
48. The Tax Dude

FOOD AND DRINK
International Food Court A
49. Fries and Things
50. Tofu-Fighters
51. Burrito Town
52. Curry By Murray
53. The Lard Yard
54. Big Cone
55. Schnecken City

International Food Court B
56. Moo Shu Fork
57. Fondue Factory
58. Pastrami Prince
59. The All-American Toasting Company
60. Lord of the Pies
61. Chicken Finger Fiesta
62. The Deep Fry

ENTERTAINMENT
63. Megamultiplex Theatres 1-16
64. Mesmerized! A Video Arcade
65. Ball, Block, and Baby
66. Bust-A-Gut Komedy Klub
67. Hole in Fun Mini-Golf
68. Van's Video Rental and Pawnshop
69. Shop 'n' Scream Indoor Roller Coaster

AMENITIES
70. Ladies' Lounge
71. Men's Room
72. Kinetic sculpture
73. Mall Walkers' Meeting Place (7:00 A.M.: weekdays)
74. Cash Machines
75. Giant bumblebee handing out flyers
76. Executive Offices
77. Fountain Full of Pennies
78. Escalators
79. Shuttle Service to Outer Ring Parking Lots
80. First Aid
81. Atrium of Relaxation
82. Lost and Found—Objects
83. Lost and Found—Children
84. Welcome Desk
85. Good-Bye Desk

PARKING
86. Outdoor parking
87. Long-term parking
88. Handicapped parking
89. Valet parking
90. Parking garage
91. Parking annex
92. Parking hangar
93. Outer ring parking lots
94. Additional parking

This map is also available in Spanish, French, Japanese, Arabic, Esperanto, and Spanglish.

Note: Map not to scale

LAWNDALE HIGH SCHOOL

HIGH SECURITY FOR HIGH PERFORMANCE

TO: LAWNDALE FACULTY AND STUDENTS

FROM: ANGELA LI, PRINCIPAL

A serious breach of school security has come to my attention. Someone has stolen the "World's Greatest Disciplinarian" figurine from my desk. This is the most blatant act of academic anarchy since last year's unfortunate computer-hacking incident, which caused an unusually large percentage of our senior class to be admitted to Ivy League universities. (I am happy to say that most of the offending students have been discovered and are back with us this year to complete remedial math.)

Now, contrary to rumor, I'm not planning to run willy-nilly over the rights of students (recent Supreme Court decisions prevent me from doing so), but beginning Monday, the following *completely legal* procedures will be implemented:

1. Surveillance cameras will be installed at strategic locations. (Note: Obscene gestures directed at the lens will be grounds for suspension.)

2. Voluntary urinalysis of all students will be instituted. Sign up now and receive a free fanny pack. Members of school athletic teams have no choice in the matter. (See <u>Veronia School District 47J vs. Acton</u> if you don't believe me.)

3. Criminologically trained dogs will be visiting our school. Please do not pet them or otherwise interfere with their work.

4. Our biweekly Bomb Scare Drills will now occur weekly.

5. A reminder: Fraternizing with security guards is strictly prohibited. I am referring, of course, to students. (Faculty members, I can't tell you what to do on your own free time, but let's not have a hormonal heyday on school property.)

6. Bathroom graffiti will be subject to handwriting analysis.

7. Vapor detectors are currently being installed. They can detect certain *fragrant* substances at one part per billion.

8. Peripheral security checks will be beefed up. You will receive your secret password in the mail shortly.

9. From now on, all chairs will be bolted to the floor.

10. The Latin Club is disbanded until further notice due to subversive activities. Thanks to the Greek Club for pointing out the circumstantial evidence.

11. The janitor will no longer be leaving his big ring of jangly keys lying around.

12. Any mention of the ACLU will severely try my patience.

To pay for these changes, the new-textbook budget has been cut in half.

Thank you for your cooperation. Let's hope all goes smoothly. Remember: A secure student is a happy student.

Angela Li

Ms. Angela Li
Principal

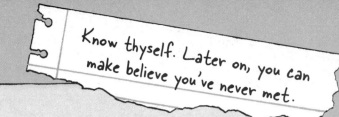

Know thyself. Later on, you can make believe you've never met.

"The road to college starts with self-knowledge."

Educational Coaching Systems

The following worksheet will help you define your personal goals and aspirations. This information will prove invaluable when choosing a college and composing an application essay. Be honest—there are no right or wrong answers, only answers that admissions officers like or dislike.

Your name: Daria Morgendorffer

1. Who I really am: I have always believed myself to be a royal princess snatched from her golden cradle by a band of rogue suburbanites.

2. Who I aspire to be: A vengeful queen.

3. What special quality do I value in myself?
My long, sensitive fingers are perfectly suited to a career in safecracking.

4. Do I prefer to spend time alone or as part of a group?
Alone—unless the group in question is made up of worshipful sycophants.

5. Favorite hobbies and interests: Drag racing; light opera.

6. Major accomplishment: Lifting a car above my head with one hand.

7. Biggest disappointment: Wings melted when I flew too close to the sun.

8. What is the neatest thing about myself? My sock drawer.

9. Who is my role model? My parents. They are living proof that the insane can lead productive lives.

10. What do I want out of my college education? A diploma.

If teachers really had eyes in the back of their heads, school would be a lot cooler.

HEY DARIA!
WHAT'S THE ANSWER TO NUMBER 215? KEVIN

There is no number 215.

That's the date.

BRITTANY-
CAN YOU COME OVER
TONITE TO "STUDY"?
KEVIN

Sorry babe.
I've got homework
to do!

DARIA CAN YOU MAKE ANY SENSE
OUT OF MRS. BENNETT'S DIAGRAM? JANE

I think the X's are consumers, and the O's
represent consumer-eating dinosaurs. But
I could be wrong.

UPCHUCK STOP SHOOTING SPITBALLS AT
ME OR I'LL RIP YOUR LUNGS OUT.
JANE.

Darling-Those aren't
spitballs...they're delicate
projectiles
of love.

Brittaneeee! My Dad's out of town.
How about a slumber party?
Charles Ruttheimer III
In your dreams, loser!
You already are! Ewwwwww!!!!

Jodie - Doesn't Kevin look extra cute today? Brit!

Maybe it's the way the fluorescent light
reflects off his hair. -J

YO! MACK DADDY! I GOT NOTHIN TO DO TONITE. HOW ABOUT COMING OVER TO WATCH THE PIGSKIN CHANNEL?
KEVIN
I'LL PASS. JODIE AND I ARE studying.
P.S. And don't call me Mack Daddy!
STUDYING? YEAH!
ALL RIGHT!!! GO MACK DADDY!!!!
What the Hell ARE you Talking About?
eeeeee-ah! My Dad is out of town
How about a slumber party?
CR III
In your dreams.
And my nightmares.

LAWNDALE HIGH SCHOOL

HIGH SECURITY FOR HIGH PERFORMANCE

REQUEST FOR PARENT/TEACHER CONFERENCE
Name of student: Daria Morgendopler
Reason: __ cutting class __ drop in grades __ tardiness
__ weapons possession _X_ other (see below)

Dear Mr. and Mrs. Morgendopler,

Your daughter, Daria, is a fine student who maintains excellent grades. But grades are only one indicator dial on the dashboard of student well-adjustedness. I fear that Daria's strong sense of irony masks a deeper, more serious malaise. (Our interaction this very afternoon was typically "charged": When I inquired as to whether she had enjoyed today's lesson, her reply of "Truly, madly, deeply" did not strike me as sincere. And earlier, when I suggested she "take one sheet and pass the rest back," she took one piece of paper and passed the rest back to ME—what could be a more clear-cut cry for help?)

Daria's reliance on sarcasm as a mode of interpersonal communication threatens to lead to detachment from her own feelings and those of others. I do not wish to alarm you, but the "ironic distance" so prevalent in our popular culture may be a more dangerous influence on our young people than all the sex and violence on television and in underwear ads combined. I believe that while Daria may be using her wit as a "defense mechanism," it often gives the impression of being a weapon, hurting those who are only trying to help—yours truly for one. Yes, Mr. and Mrs. Morgendopler, I am not ashamed to admit that sometimes, after a conversation with Daria...I ache.

If I take a special interest in Daria, it is because she reminds me of myself at a young age, before I discovered Gestalt and the writings of M. Scott Peck. Can we set up a meeting at your earliest convenience to discuss this matter? It would mean so much to your daughter's future and my own sense of self-worth.

Sincerely,

Mr. O'Neill

Timothy O'Neill
Lawndale High School
English/Language Arts/Dramatic Horizons/Self-Esteem Workshop

Dear Mr. O'Neill:

Regarding your correspondence concerning my daughter Daria and her "sarcasm": What color is the sky in YOUR world? Do you seriously expect me to discourage in a young woman the very coping mechanisms that will allow her to succeed in today's dog-eat-dog professional environment—one that demands dispassionate action over mushy emotionalism?

This is the third note you have sent home re your vague touchy-feely notions of proper social behavior. At your request, I did speak to Daria about her "attitude," and she assured me that her comments were hardly malicious, simply insightful. I regret that you found the truth to be painful, though if you spend all your time telling yourself that you're really, really all right after all, no wonder it comes as a shock to meet someone with a different opinion. I understand where you're coming from: I too have come to superficial realizations while hugging complete strangers on mountaintops. But it's time you acknowledge that this is the nineties. I believe your job is to teach my daughter about literature. If you want to hang out a therapist's shingle, do so on your own time. As a lawyer, I can assure you that in this state you do not need to pass any difficult licensing exams or earn any additional degrees in order to do so. Even if you can't get something as simple as a STUDENT'S LAST NAME right.

Best regards,

Helen Morgendorffer

Helen Morgendorffer

DICTATED BUT NOT READ

cc: Jake Morgendorffer

Behind My Eyelids
by Trent Lane

As lashes close
I see my woes
Spread out like a carpet of bugs
In absence of light
Pass visions of night
~~As snug as a bug in a rug~~   Already used "bugs"!
And shallow graves left halfway dug

Behind my eyelids
Is a world you cannot see
A place that's just for me
Behind my eyelids

You watch a tear
It trickles clear
And glistens on my skin
~~Corn is a grain~~ My liquid pain
~~It grows on the plain~~ Oh, world profane
Please, baby, let me in.

        Repeat chorus

reamin
(rain)

(grain)

rain
Spain
mainly
(plain)
plane
stain
insane
membrane
(profane)

Wayne

light
sprite
bite
white
blight
flight
night

uptight
kite
ignite
in-flight
parasite
~~dike~~

Trent—
Really cool. Lot of emotion.
Where's the guitar solo go?

                    Jesse

From the Futon
by Trent Lane

There's no place to hide things
Under the bed
And nowhere to hide from what's true
Down here by the floor
My soul calls out "More!"
But knows that its cry won't get through

From the futon
From the futon
Everything, always so low
From the futon
From the futon
I'm in limbo—how low can I go?

I don't have a headboard
Or box spring of wire
My spirit's hit low altitude
The mattress is thin
It's itching my skin
And that isn't helping my mood

From the futon
From the futon

Everything, always so low
From the futon
From the futon
I'm in limbo—how low can I go?

Trent—
You're a genius!

Can I sing it?

thin
tin
spin
sin
chin
Mannequin
paraffin

BUXTON RIDGE MILITARY ACADEMY

FOUNDED 1909
READING, WRITING AND REGIMENTATION

Dear Mom and Dad,

My first week at military school was good, except they make you get up at six a.m., even if you're tired because you stayed up all night holding it in because you were afraid to go to the bathroom (not me—someone else). We have letter writing now from 20:15 to 20:25 (that's military time, which goes higher than normal time). I have a stiff upper lip, like you told me to. The Commandant said something about breaking my spirit. I have one friend. His name is Randy, and he is here because he put his fist through a wall. He is a good pal to have. He asked me why I was here, and I told him I don't know. Please tell me, so I won't do it again. One of the other guys told me they censor the letters just like in the real Army, but I think he's a ████████ ████████ I have an important job: I am on the laundry squad. I will try to make you proud. If I make you proud, can I come home soon?

Your son,

Jake

BUXTON RIDGE MILITARY ACADEMY

FOUNDED 1909
READING, WRITING AND REGIMENTATION

Dear Mom and Dad,

Thanks for the care package. I'm sure I would have enjoyed it, but it was confiscated because it had the incorrect zip code and you used the wrong kind of tape (at least that's what they told me. But I think Colonel ████ swiped it because he could smell the pecan nougat rolls). I am moving up in the ranks and am no longer a plebe. The big guys don't hang me from the flagpole by my underwear anymore, but sometimes they still make me eat my dress socks for fun. As you can see from the picture, I am part of the color guard. I slipped on the wet grass this morning and messed up the formation, so they made me move a big pile of dirt from one place to another, and then move it back. (You explain it to me. Just try.) I have thigh burns from rappelling, and I've been breaking out in really weird rashes. There are no girls and you have ruined my life. See you on visiting day.

Your son, Jake

FOUNDED 1909
READING, WRITING AND REGIMENTATION

Dear Mom and Dad,

   Here I am on the Leadership Platoon Reaction
Course. Yes, they've made a man out of me—a man
forever scarred by soul-crushing humiliations.
It's been four years of living ███. You're
going to force me to stay here, aren't you? I've
got 98 demerits, but they still won't kick me
out. They just make me march around the bullring
for four hours straight every day. Randy went
AWOL—I would have gone with him, but why give
you the satisfaction, Dad? You would never let
me forget it. Well, I'll show you. If I've
learned anything here, it's how to control my
anger and use it to fuel an unending resentment.
I'm going to stay the course and graduate so that
you can never hold my failure against me. After
that, somehow, someway, I will make you pay.
(Mom: I know this whole thing wasn't your idea—
you never could stand up to Dad.)

Love,

Jake

FOUNDED 1909
READING, WRITING AND REGIMENTA

Dear Mom and Dad,

Do you like my shiny shoes? I polished them with my
own spit. This is me with my date from the Military
Ball. Her name is Eileen and her dad owns a gas
station. From this picture, you would never know that
she had three other escorts that evening. (The girls
in this town have it made.) You realize, of course,
that when I come of age, you can no longer tell me
what to do. I'm splitting for the coast and you can't
stop me. My days of structured discipline and
sacrificial teamwork are over. I plan to ████ and
████ and ████ like all those flower children I see
on the news. Ha ha, just kidding! I'm glad we made
up, Dad, and you made that tuition payment to
Middleton College! I really plan to hit the books
next year! Too bad I can't be with all my good
friends when they ship off to 'Nam.

Your son, Jake Morgendorffer

Copy Forwarded to
COMMANDANT OF CADETS

Brittany is smarter than she looks. But it would be hard not to be.

DEAR BRITTANY

An expert answers your questions about life, love, and lipstick

Dear Brittany,
Do opposites really attract?

Just Wondering

Dear Wondering,
Opposites attract, but so do sames. And sometimes it's better to date a guy you have things in common with—and I don't just mean your lips line up. Otherwise you might end up waiting around at a boat show for four hours while he looks at stupid old motors, and then you'll probably have a fight and ruin your makeup. Dumb quarterback jerk.

Dear Brittany,
I like the same guy as my best friend. What should I do?

Feeling Guilty

Dear Guilty,
I'd go for the guy. Once you have a boyfriend, you don't have much time to hang out with other girls, anyway.

Dear Brittany,
I like a boy from a rival football team. He likes me back. But if we get together, I'm afraid I will lose all my friends and I will have to quit the cheerleading squad.

Torn Between Two Lineups

Dear Torn,
This sounds just like my favorite play, Romeo and Juliet, *except that hopefully you don't both die in the end. And Shakespeare didn't have any cheerleaders in his play, because there weren't any back then. And football players don't wear tights. Actually, they do, in a way. What was the question? Oh, yeah, you should follow your heart, but don't tell anyone at school. And if they find out, you can always say you were on a spy mission. (And I hope you're not talking about a certain Oakwood quarterback who has a black convertible with red leather seats, because it may turn out that he was just using you, not that I would know.)*

Dear Brittany,
You are so smart, maybe you can help me. I have a really great boyfriend, but sometimes he doesn't give me all the attention I deserve. He spends way too much time at football practice and watching the Pigskin Channel. He doesn't get it that a woman needs to feel special, and a great way to make her feel special is to buy her jewelry. What should I do?

Taken for Granted

Dear Taken,
You sound like a super terrific girl who should be treated much better, especially by a guy who is lucky to be going out with you at all. Maybe he is super cute, but you could be going out with someone who is just a little less cute and maybe you will. I think your boyfriend should shape up fast. If he were reading this now—which he better be, the dumb quarterback jerk—he would realize that he should take you someplace extra nice this weekend and beg for forgiveness because otherwise he's going to be yesterday's lunch.

Do *you* have a question for Brittany? Type or print clearly, on the cutest stationery you can find, using simple sentences and words that everyone knows, and send your question to: **ASK BRITTANY** c/o THE LAWNDALE LOWDOWN.

[5]

Life in Lawndale is as exciting as ever. That's the problem.

My family is active and busy. Mom has thrown herself into home and work, except for the home part. Dad has thrown himself into reading the paper at the table. Quinn has threatened to throw herself in front of a train if she's not allowed to date on weeknights.

I've got the daily routine down pretty well now. Go to school, avoid making eye contact with teachers, get called on anyway. Walk halls between classes, be ignored by other students. Go home, listen to parents' frantic messages on answering machine about working late, watch TV. It's a good life. I just hope I can keep up the frenetic pace.

Occasionally I think about doing something to change my situation, but where am I going to get hold of a Stealth bomber?

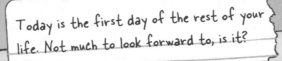
CAREER CLIMBER

WEEK OF
OCT 19 - OCT 25

OCT 19: SUNDAY
Afternoon quality time with Dana (this time must stay cool!)

Train for Corporate Fun Run while strategizing
Garcia partial-spleen-removal strategy

Library Board meeting (handicapped-parking brouhaha)

OCT 20: MONDAY
Breakfast powwow: Peterson scar-tissue liability case

Have Marianne send navy pumps out for reheeling

Call Rita and Amy about who's getting Mother
for the holidays

OCT 21: TUESDAY
Eric out of office (hers with Carl?)
Marianne at coffee-brewing seminar from 2 to 4

Post-dinner Family Court: Family v. Jake Morgenscriffer
(re: carpet wear in living room--bring pacing photos)

OCT 22: WEDNESDAY
Sensitivity training
Don't forget to subpoena night watchman
Dinner with Mike Patrick and wife (name?)-pump
him for his take on drive-through laser eye surgery

OCT 23: THURSDAY
Relationship adviser-7 A.M.-Tell Jake!

Sewage slip-and-fall rebriefing

Start upper-arm exercise regimen

OCT 24: FRIDAY
Have Marianne get winter Chanel out of cold storage

Go to bed early and get a good night's sleep

Set alarm for 3 A.M. call with Tokyo office

OCT 25: SATURDAY
Pre-fun Run focusing with Madame Sala
Corporate Fun Run-3 P.M.
(don't forget change of clothes!)
Post-fun Run cocktail party at Chantal's
(never enough focus--eat on the way)

BUSY FELLA™

SUNDAY OCTOBER 19
Meet with tree surgeon-cut down infested maple?
Torch bugs afterward?
Round of golf-Pete, Andrew, Ray. Wear lucky green pants
Helen at meeting cook dinner for the girls (fish sticks?)

MONDAY OCTOBER 20
Review sales chart data
Get computer guy to make sales charts colorful
3 p.m.: dentist-discuss teeth grinding

TUESDAY OCTOBER 21
New phone-conference-system training
(find out what red button does)
Meet with direct-mail team about cost of personalized stickers
Stupid family court thing-dammit!

WEDNESDAY OCTOBER 22
Entertainment Symposium-Margate Hotel Bayside
Sign off on Mr. Pecan Web site budget
Dinner with Mike Patrick and wife (name?)
(let HIM reach for check!)

BUSY FELLA™

THURSDAY OCTOBER 23
Morning free!!! 7 a.m.:damn marriage counselor
Phone conference with new salad-dressing strategist
7 p.m.: accountant (mountain bike-business expense?)

FRIDAY OCTOBER 24
Proven Profits breakfast (ask Helen what to wear)
Mom's birthday-leave message on her machine
Both girls out of house tonight - wear silk boxers

SATURDAY OCTOBER 25
Gutter-cleaning estimate (like he's really gonna show up)
Watch Helen in Fun Run-take thermos full of screwdrivers
Yet one more party with a bunch of uptight phonies

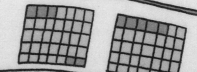

Teen Runner

Sunday, Oct. 19

CUTE TREE GUY!!!
Dinner with Dad and Daria [chance to convince
Dad that Mom was wrong about double-dating
without another girl]
Alphabetize nail polish colors

Monday, Oct. 20

Before History - ask Daria who won Civil War
Start of new dating cycle (T-Z)
Fashion Club after-school debate with
Oakwood: Spiral Curls versus the Straight-
Haired Look

Tuesday, Oct. 21

Change name to Starr?
Family Court (get excused for reading
books to old blind people)
Date with Taylor- Chez Pierre

Wednesday, Oct. 22

English test: Rent that Demi Moore movie
about the lady with the embroidery on her shirt
Fashion Club - group pedicure
Ask Joey, Jeffy, or that other one to drive
me to and from date with Will

Thursday, Oct. 23

Find out if Sandi still intends to wear that
crop top we both have
Return pearl earrings to Mom and borrow
diamond studs
Baby-sit Gupty kids -- bring pants for Tad
to shorten

Friday, Oct. 24

Batting practice -- bring mascara
Update locker posters
Date with Zach - Casa Alejandro

Saturday, Oct. 25

Rotate hangers
Meet Fashion Club at mall for holiday
chignon demonstration at Cashman's
Date with Alejandro [new dating cycle A-E]

Oct. 19: Sunday
"Quality Time" with Mom.
    (Bring up taking a year off from school)
Dad's lousy fish sticks
Bad Movie Night at Jane's

Oct. 20: Monday
Bring in diorama of Haymarket Riot
Avoid school-play tryouts
        Mail form to reserve place at
        Bigfoot convention

Oct. 21: Tuesday
        Oral presentation for DeMartino's class:
"Failed Utopian Communities"
Family Court—invite Jane over to practice being a
courtroom sketch artist
Study for French test: Read Tintin comics

Oct. 22: Wednesday
Check on slime-mold experiment—update charts, add
oatmeal flakes
8 PM—check out new TV show—Poor Pathetic
Planet
Leave depressed poem around for Mom to find

Oct. 23: Thursday
Art class field trip to museum (forget glasses)
Log onto Area 51 chat room posing as someone who
gives a damn
Cut Quinn down to size

Oct. 24: Friday
Deadline for literary magazine—knock out something
meaningful for extra credit
Mr. O'Neill's every-other-Friday surprise quiz
Check Forecast Channel for new tornado footage

Oct. 25: Saturday
Last day of Carnivorous Plant
Expo

(Mom and Dad at Fun Run:
explore dresser drawers?)

Sleep over at Jane's (bring own
pajamas this time)

Homepage: Get Out of Your Rutt!

The Charles Ruttheimer III
Homepage

ULTRASUAVE UNIVERSE

* **GALLERY OF FEISTY BABES**
Click here for my picks: la crème de les frisky femmes.

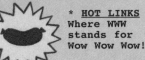

* **HOT LINKS**
Where WWW stands for Wow Wow Wow!

* **THE SHEMP HOWARD SEARCH ENGINE (UNDER CONSTRUCTION)**
It's a big job, but someone's gotta do it.

NEW! * **MAKE-OUT MUSIC**
Dim the lights and download these sexy song snippets.

* **PHOTO GALLERY**
A little something for the ladies—downloadable pictures of yours truly. (G-rated...yet enticing!)

* **PICK-UP LINE ARCHIVE**
Contributions from around the globe. Maintained as a public service.

* **JOKES I HEARD IN HOMEROOM**
Updated daily. (Warning: Some off-color material.)

NEW! * **CHARLES'S COLLECTIBLES CORNER**
My collection of fast-food premiums: Search by date, character, restaurant, movie tie-in.

email: Contact me at mrfine@ultrasuave.com

URL: www.ultrasuave.com/welcome.html

Babes Ahoy!

Charles Ruttheimer III Presents:
THE GALLERY OF FEISTY BABES

AGENT SCULLY
X-citing! I'm no
skeptic...she's as
feisty as they come!

ELEANOR ROOSEVELT
Not "hot," but just
try denying she was
feisty—you cannot!

AEON FLUX
Best-dressed
animated gal.
I love her
feistiness...
so shoot me!

TERI HATCHER
Not as feisty as
the competition,
but who am I to argue
with Superman?
Click here for
<u>Teri GIFs.</u>

PRINCESS LEIA
You don't need
The Force when
you're feisty!

MYSTERY LADY
I fear she'd kill
me if I revealed
her identity.
Now that's feisty!

Nominate a candidate: email to: feistygal@ultrasuave.com

Back to <u>Ultrasuave Universe Home</u>

Connect: host: *www.ultrasuave.com/feisty.htm*

Hot Links

Charles Ruttheimer III's Favorite Web Pages

* <u>Bikini Island Catalog</u>
Escape to a tropical
paradise. Like a Jimmy
Buffett song without
Jimmy Buffett—the best
kind!

* <u>Monty Python Trivia
Quiz</u>
Over 1,000 questions. I
won't tell you my score,
for it would make you
feel inadequate.

* <u>Captain Muscle FAQ</u>
Complete origins of all
three parallel
universes!

* <u>Virtual Tour of the
Playboy Mansion Grotto</u>
Circa 1964. (I hear
it's pretty dull there
since Hef got hitched.)
Do try the "Shoot Your
Way Out" game!

* <u>Association de
l'Apprèciation de
Jerry Lewis</u>
In French. But you will
enjoy it, since le Jerry
speaks the universal
language of laughter.

* <u>Coffeepot Cam</u>
Real-time feed of coffee
brewing. Strangely
compelling.

* <u>soc.history.brassiere</u>
The only newsgroup I read
regularly. Fascinating
debates.

Back to
<u>Ultrasuave Universe Home</u>

URL: *www.ultrasuave.com/hotlinks.htm*

To: All Field Trip Participants

From: Ms. Defoe

Our trip to the County Museum of Modern Art (COMMA) will take place this Friday. The bus will leave from the school parking lot at 8:00 A.M. Bring a notebook and pen, an open mind, and a packed lunch—food available at the museum is pretty, but overpriced.

Here are some tips to make your art experience both educational and enjoyable:

<u>DO'S AND DON'TS</u>

DO pay attention to the tour guide—or at least look like you are.

DO wear your little metal button at all times.

DO keep your hands to yourself: We don't want another fiasco like last year's urn incident at the Palace of Pottery.

DO jump up and down on the front steps like Rocky. You're only young once.

DO write down how the art makes you feel. If it makes you feel nauseous, place your head between your knees and breathe deeply.

DON'T snicker at the nudes.

DON'T try to see how close you can get to the paintings without setting off the alarm.

DON'T step on anything that could be art.

DON'T ask the guard if he hates his job.

DON'T go looking for the dinosaurs—that's another museum.

DON'T pick up any "free" souvenirs in the gift shop, Kevin.

<u>THINGS TO KNOW ABOUT ART</u>

1. If it doesn't look like anything, maybe it's supposed to be an emotion.

2. If it's not an emotion either, it's "art for art's sake."

3. Believe it or not, the biggest paintings are not always worth the most money.

4. If you are puzzled by something, say "How postmodern!" and move on.

5. Sculptors are moodier than painters. (At least that's been MY experience.)

MANATEE

FOR THOSE WITH A THIRST FOR
KNOWLEDGE

MANATEE COLLEGE
SLACK ISLAND, FLORIDA
FOUNDED A.D. 1982
AVERAGE DAILY TEMPERATURE: 78° F.

Dear **Ms. Quinn Morgendorffer**,

We are pleased to inform you that you have been accepted into the undergraduate program at Manatee College. Although you have not officially applied, your reputation for first-rate studenting precedes you, and we are thrilled to offer you early admission. Your excellent work at **Lawndale High School** has so impressed us that we are confident in your ability to succeed as a member of our student body. So there is no need for you to fill out confusing forms or compose bothersome essays; simply return the RSVP card in the enclosed envelope—you don't even need a stamp!

Manatee College's beachfront accommodations and flexible academic standards* place it among the most innovative and attractive institutions of higher learning in the state of Florida. The soothing sound of rolling surf makes for a relaxing educational environment, and our poolside library contains more than 300 books and books-on-tape, many on subjects relevant to the curriculum.† Room service is available at all times.

To ensure your place in our freshman class three years from now, please respond promptly so we can begin the necessary financial background check.

Good work, **Quinn**! We can't wait to see you!

Sincerely,

Alan Morrison
Admissions Officer
and Social Director

* Manatee College offers no academic classes "per se," but instead provides valuable beachfront "life experience" for $10,000 per semester, subject to change without prior notification.
† Use of the word *curriculum* is not meant to imply the existence of an accredited degree program or programs.

Wish you were here.
We could switch places.

Hey Janey,
This open road thing rocks. Jesse and I wrote a bunch of new songs. But we're out of gas. And money. Ask Mom and Dad to send $$$ c/o Dusty's General Store, Briarback, Arizona. If they're gone again, ask somebody else's mom and dad.
Trent

Jane Lane
111 Howard Drive
Lawndale

BONE DRY
Nevada
America's Barrenest Ghost Town

Pinetop Motel
Route 17A
Haineyville, Pennsylvania
Cable TV Seasonal Rates Carpeting

MOM, DAD, JANE AND TRENT—
HAVE COURTNEY AND ADRIAN
CALLED YET? THE LOCAL POLICE
AREN'T MUCH INTERESTED.
HOW MANY TIMES AM I GOING
TO HAVE TO GO THROUGH THIS?

LOVE,
SUMMER
P.S.—I HOPE IT'S OK THAT I
DROPPED THE OTHER TWO AT
YOUR HOUSE. NO ONE WAS HOME,
SO I TOLD THEM TO WAIT.

THE LANES

111 HOWARD DRIVE

LAWNDALE

Pinetop
MOTEL

How are you?
Just want you to know
we are fine. (Oh
yeah, thanks for the
excellent Christmas
presents!) Made
some cool friends.
If you hear from Mom,
tell her to chill.
We'll call her in a
few weeks.

Careful out among
the English,

Adrian
 and Courtney

Grandpa and
Grandma Lane
111 Howard Drive
Lawnda

GREETINGS FROM AMISH COUNTRY
...IT'S JUST PLAIN FUN!

Dear Family,
Job hunting here is even
worse than in Mexico, and
they don't give a damn how
well you habla español. Of
course, I COULD get a
position if I were willing to
work for the World Bank or
become a lackey of the urban
elite. I think I'll try Honduras
instead - basketry is booming.
And I hear they have a
government.
      Vaya con Dios,
      Penny

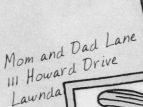

120 NICARAGUA

Mom and Dad Lane
111 Howard Drive
Lawnda

"We're Just
Itching to
See You!"

I'M
HUNGRY

NICARAGUA'S MOSQUITO COAST

Dear Kids,
The weeklong Clay Intensive is going well. You should see my urn! Can you turn off the kiln? I left it on by mistake.
Love,
Mom

P.S.: Where's your father? Any ideas?

Jane and Trent Lane
111 Howard Drive
Lawndale

LOVE
USA 25

SWEET MUD
NEW AGE SPA
...AND
CRAFTS COLONY

CLAY

Hey everybody!

Getting married again. You'd like her—her name is Sheila and she isn't like the other ones. It turns out that the guy who married me last time wasn't who he said he was, so I think this is OK legally.

Later,
Wind

RAZOR CLAM USA 25

The Lane Family
111 Howard Drive
Lawndale

The Hitch Hutch
WHERE "I DO" IS DRIVE-THRU

Kids,
The Great Cavern is everything they said and more. Six more weeks of retreat and then fire up the BBQ- Daddy's home! Love to Mom if she's there.

Dad

Jane and
    Trent Lane
111 Howard Drive
Lawndal[e]

Hey everyone!
This place is the coolest yet. The trees are made of rock!!!! And guess what- we got jobs chipping off pieces for the souvenir shop. We're saving up, and we'll probably be home for some holiday. Say hi to Mom,
Adrian and Courtney

P.S. Uncle Trent and his friend stopped by. Weird coincidence! Gave them some money from the "Need a penny/Leave a penny" cup.

P.P.S. If Mom insists on coming, tell her to bring the van. We have a dog now.

The Lanes

111 Howard Drive

Lawndale

I don't go in for male-bashing.
Why limit yourself?

WANTED: CAR POO...
CAR IMPOUNDE...
NEED RIDE!
LONG STORY
— Donati...

STUDY
SUBJECTS
NEEDED
f you are
etween the
ges of 20
nd 50 and
nd yourself
reading the
uture, you
nay be
ligible to
eceive $25
or filling out
simple
orm.
ee Ms.
lanson.

FOR SALE:
Pink taffeta
gown. Size 8.
Never worn.
Best offer.
See Ms...

FEMALE
FACULTY
ONLY!

(if any men are still reading this it just proves you ignore us when
we're talking to you and do whatever you want despite the fact that
your actions stab us in the heart.)

a meeting of
the laundale divorced women's empowerment circle
* 7:00 p.m. first wednesday of the month
* laundale women's center (above judy's jujitsu)
* frank discussion
* group venting rituals
* swap legal strategies and horror stories
* a supportive environment for healing
  constructive anger and revenge fantasies

this month's topic
women who run with scum

coming soon
payback time: how to turn in your ex to the irs
letting your gray grow in because who the hell cares anyway?
involuntary manslaughter and you
(the legally separated are welcome)
donation: two susan b. anthony dollars
(they're legal tender—don't let any man tell you otherwise)

* see ms barch for more information

F
PI

SAT
OCTO

MISSING
KEY to men's bathroom
(attached to large plastic
buttplate) Return to office
immedi...
IRRESPONSIBLE
MALES!

Superfine AquaGreen Algae
Nutritious Vitamin Drink
Make money and do good
at the same time.
See Mr. O'Neill for
info pack.

Due 3/20
This week's assignment is to write a short story in which your main
character overcomes adversity and learns a valuable lesson. Remember: To
receive a passing grade, you must utilize both simile AND metaphor. Don't

THE MALEVOLENT SECRET OF HADDON HALL
By Daria Morgendorffer

I arrived at Haddon Hall a lonely, bereft orphan. My reprobate father
had left my innocent mother for a small-waisted dance-hall girl, and the
saintly soul had gone insane and thrown herself into the swirling Thames.
My father was later found strangled with a stocking.

Do you really need this detail?

I was a desperate animal, shaking with fear and hunger. My shoes
were caked with mud and my brow flushed with fever. As thunder roared
around me, a jagged streak of lightning ripped through the sky and struck a
massive oak tree. It cracked in two and fell, landing inches from where I
stood. Was this a foreshadowing of things to come?

I had been summoned by the mysterious and reclusive Monsieur La
Forge, who had agreed to take me in upon learning of my parents' untimely
demise. Rumor has it that my mother (whom I resemble to an astonishing
degree) had spurned his affections years before. But what was his interest
in me?

I felt misgivings, but...anything for a free meal, I always say.

The door creaked open and a ghostly, wizened face appeared. "You
must be Eliza. Enter. Monsieur has been expecting you."

I followed the hunched and ancient form into a dank, dusty room,
draped with velvet curtains and ablaze with the light of dozens of candles.

Monsieur La Forge stood with his back to me. When he spun around, I
could not help but gasp: His teeth came to ivory points, and his eyes were
bright yellow and feline in appearance. Bloodstains dotted his shirt.

My pulse quickened. Something was not right.

So I pulled the wooden stake from under my bodice and thrust it deep
into his chest. And a few well-placed kicks to the gut disabled the creaky
old geezer. Then I cut off his head just to be on the safe side.

For you see, my meek appearance belies an observant nature.

And I always carry a wooden stake when venturing into unfamiliar
surroundings of a Gothic nature. I'm no dummy.

I tore the bejeweled pendant from the dead vampire's neck
and began compiling a mental list of reliable pawnshops. If I hurried

I'd like to be popular—if it didn't require having other people like you.

WAIF Magazine Asks:

HOW POPULAR ARE YOU?

There's more to life than being popular, but when you're popular, everything else is so much easier! If you're a regular reader of WAIF (and have been following our beauty advice and personality tips), you're probably pretty popular already. But how can you be sure? Take our simple test and find out!

1. What qualities do you look for in a friend?
A. Sense of humor, character, and intelligence.
B. Someone who won't steal my boyfriend.
C. Nice hair, expensive car, perfect eyebrow arch.

2. How would you describe the ideal guy?
A. A sincere person who accepts me and loves me for who I am.
B. He shows up.
C. His family has a different house for each season.

3. My social circle is made up of:
A. People I like and want to get to know better.
B. People I like and want to get to know so they'll invite me to parties.
C. People I don't like, but I want everyone else to know I hang out with.

4. How big is your closet?
A. I've never measured it.
B. Less than 36 cubic feet.
C. More than 36 cubic feet.*

*If you need help measuring, ask your math tutor or a cute guy.

5. How often do you date?
A. A lot.
B. Quite a lot.
C. As much as humanly possible.

6. How do you treat people who are less popular than you?
A. Like everyone else.
B. I make believe I don't see them.
C. I don't have to make believe, since I really DON'T see them.

7. How do you treat people who are more popular than you are?
A. Like everyone else.
B. Better than everyone else.
C. There aren't any.

8. How important are good grades?
A. Very: I find it rewarding to succeed academically.
B. Somewhat: Otherwise my parents will ground me.
C. Extremely: Or I could end up at some community college without fraternities or a decent football team.

9. When you invite someone to a party, they usually say...
A. "Uh...thanks."
B. "I'd love to come."
C. "This is the greatest day of my life!"

10. Imagine you have an unpopular sister. What do you do?
A. Tell her I love her whether she is popular or not.
B. Encourage her to be friendly and outgoing.
C. Ask my parents to put her up for adoption.

$$
\begin{array}{rr}
2 & +1 \\
+2 & 2 \\
2 & 2 \\
2 & 2 \\
2 & +2 \\
\hline
& 19
\end{array}
$$

WOMEN SEEKING MEN

PURRRFECT FOR YOU
Our owner is a positive and perky SWF (30s—looks 20s). She seeks a SM (40s—looks 30s), who loves adorable kitties like us, to fall in love with FUR-ever! Someone in a helping profession preferred. No emotional baggage or dogs. Note and catnip toy to: Box 5556. Meow.

SOS!
DBCNSNDPRM CEO, 43. ISO SW/B/ANSNDPRF for TLC and LTR. Loves: REM, NFL, G&T's. Hates: NIN, ABFAB, ASCAP. No AA/NA/SA or NRA. Box 3436.

SLEEPLESS IN SUBURBIA
Attractive, vivacious SF, 40ish, seeks a smart, mature man with *joie de vivre*. My interests include: literature, long walks on the beach, cooking, holding hands. I'm a pushover for a good-looking pair of feet! Note and photo to: Box 4848. Please be real.

ARE YOU FOR ME?
SWF with nasty attitude seeks love slave to bow to my will in sleazy motel rooms. Interests: Sunday picnics in the park, *The Simpsons*. Box 3890.

ANTHONY DEMARTINO

Dear Miss Box-holder 4848,

I was intrigued by your ad. Although I rarely venture out amongst the brutish hordes who haunt the cookie-cutter chain restaurants and booze-drenched meat markets that pass themselves off as social gathering places during these waning days of our civilization, I, too, am hoping to meet that certain special someone to cuddle.

I differ from the common testosterone-pumping behemoth you might encounter in that I am at peace with myself. I enjoy a quiet night at home with a good book, a roast chicken, and the toes of my two well-formed feet comfortably wiggling about in my prized whirlpool foot massager. All I need is the right woman to complete the picture.

I am a SWM, 48, svelte, with salt-and-pepper hair and intense good looks. I am magnetic, honest (perhaps too much so) and of intelligence far above average. When you meet me, you will see that these things are true. I demand much from myself and others. Some find me brusque, but inside I am a warm, caring individual who merely, sadly, finds the majority of other people on the planet to be exasperatingly slow-witted.

I am an educator by profession and a philosopher by temperament. I have never been married, although I did co-habitate back in my "beatnik" days. We are still friends, although we have not spoken in years.

At your leisure, please write to me at the address below. I hope to meet you soon to attempt intimacy.

Respectfully yours,

Anthony DeMartino

210 Barker Drive
Lawndale

Fashion Club Minutes

Written down by Stacy, secretary.

February

Would have read the minutes from the last meeting, but I spilled diet soda on them. Sandi gave a presentation on "Overcoming Your Fear of Horizontal Stripes," which was very informational. Discussed whether to open the club up to more members. Concluded that we should keep it exclusive so people have something to strive for. Debated which fastener we like best: zippers, buttons, or snaps? Decided more research was needed. Agreed that Quinn was right to tell Paula Parsky that you can see her black underwear through her white pants: will do even more community service from now on. Reviewed our request to Ms. Li asking for work/study credit for window-shopping. Ate some carrot and celery sticks. Then took care of unresolved business: decided Sandi SHOULD go back and buy the canary-yellow sling-backs with the cork-heel platforms that she put on hold at Cashman's. Meeting ended early so Quinn could make a 4:15 appointment to get her split ends trimmed.

March

Meeting called to order by Quinn, since Sandi was stuck at home recovering from a twisted ankle caused by falling off her shoes. Read the minutes from last month: Quinn asked that the split ends thing be struck from the record. I said I'd think about it. Voted that we would not wear emerald green on St. Patrick's Day since none of us is Irish and we all look sick in colors that have too much yellow in them. Will wear blue-green and hope no one notices. Quinn asked if Tiffany and I thought Sandi was doing a good job as President—not that she was saying she WASN'T, but did we think Sandi really meant that stuff about horizontal stripes or was she just setting us up? We said we thought Sandi was a GREAT President. Then Quinn got all nervous and asked me if I write down EVERYTHING we say and if I do, could I erase what she just said about Sandi? I told her that would be like going back in time, which is impossible. Then she said "but what about white patent-leather boots? What about the disco revival?" Then I said, "That's not the same thing as going back in time, that's just reinterpreting classic apparel concepts." So then SHE said

It's great that my family likes to read. It cuts down on all that useless conversation.

Lying here on my bed, staring at a fascinating crack in the ceiling, I consider the past year. I've left a place where I don't fit in and moved to a whole new place where I don't fit in. I've made a new friend who is equally unpopular, so that together we really drive people away. And, thankfully, I can always count on my family...to make me want to join the Witness Protection Program. Yes, things have really improved in the last twelve months. By which I mean they haven't gotten any worse.

At least keeping this journal has been a valuable experience. Maybe I flatter myself, but I think I could be a professional writer if I put my mind to it. A bitter, angry hack who starts fistfights at cocktail parties—I could do that job.

Anyway, the sun is setting, the moon is rising, and I can hear the lonesome sigh of the wind outside my window—no, wait, that's Quinn's blow dryer. The future is an enormous question mark, and I don't know what lies ahead. I only know that if it moves, I'm shooting it.

Daria